Originally published as *Mila en haar vriendjes* in Belgium and the Netherlands by Clavis Uitgeverij, 2015
English translation from the Dutch by Clavis Publishing Inc., New York

Visit us on the Web at www.clavis-publishing.com.

Mila and Her Friends written by Judith Koppens and illustrated by Anouk Nijs

ISBN 978-1-60537-744-5

This book was printed in March 2022 at Wai Man Book Binding (China) Ltd. Flat A, 9/F.,
Phase I, Kwun Tong Industrial Centre, 472-484 Kwun Tong Road, Kwun Tong, Kowloon, H.K.

First Edition
10 9 8 7 6 5 4 3 2 1

Written by Judith Koppens
Illustrated by Anouk Nijs

Mila
and Her Friends

Clavis

NEW YORK

My name is **Mila**. Some days I live with my daddy, and some days I live with my mommy. Today I'm staying at Daddy's. He picks me up from school. "Hi, Mila," Daddy says happily. "Did you have fun at school?"

I walk straight to Daddy. "Daddy, look!
These are my new friends.
They're called Sam and Liza.
Can they come over to play at our house?"
Sam and Liza give Daddy a sweet smile.

"Of course they can, Mila," Daddy says.
"But first we have to check with Sam's and Liza's mommies to see if they think it's okay."
"Sure," the mommies say. "We'll come and pick you up later. Have fun!"

"Come on, little monsters," Daddy jokes.
"Let's go and have fun." He picks up Sam
and Liza, and he gives me a piggyback ride.
Sam and Liza scream with laughter.
My silly daddy makes me laugh too.

"First we'll have something to eat," Daddy says.
"What do little monsters eat?" Liza, Sam, and I think.
"Monster pancakes with strawberry jam, of course!"
Daddy cries. Yummy! My friends and I sure love those!

After the pancakes, Daddy takes the hair gel from the bathroom. "Monsters have monster hair, of course," he says.

Daddy puts gel in our hair. It glitters! Sam looks in the mirror and starts laughing. "It looks dangerous. Roar!" he shouts.

Daddy goes to the box with dress-up clothes.
"Monsters have monster clothes, of course."
"And they walk like monsters too!" Liza shrieks while
she makes silly monster moves with her arms and legs.
My friends and I walk around the room like real
monsters. Do you see that monster daddy
over there?

"Grumble, grumble," Sam growls.
He has green monster ears and silly monster feet.
"Monsters make monster sounds!"
Liza and I growl like real monsters now too.
And Daddy? He joins in!

Ding-dong!
The doorbell rings.
We run with big
monster steps
to the door . . .

and there are
Liza's and Sam's
mommies!

"What happened to you?"
Sam's mommy says, surprised.

Liza's mommy is
standing with her hand over
her mouth and doesn't say a word.

It's quiet for a while.
"Er . . ." Daddy says. "These are monsters,
with monster hair and monster clothes."

"And they're very good at
one thing," Daddy says while
he winks at us and pushes
Liza and Sam forward.
"They give the best . . ."

"Monster cuddles!"
Liza and Sam cuddle with their mommies
and make sweet monster sounds.
"Grumble, grumble, grumble!"
And that makes the mommies laugh.

"Bye, monster friends!" I shout.

"Bye, monster Mila! Bye, monster daddy!"
Liza and Sam shout.

"See you tomorrow
at school!
Playing together
was fun!"